For Honor

So Cosy

Lerryn Korda

WALKER BOOKS
AND SUBSIDIARIES
LONDON · BOSTON · SYDNEY · AUCKLAND

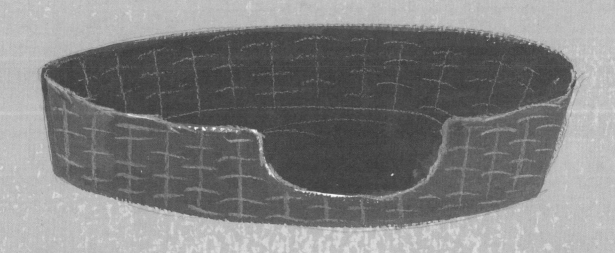

Dog snuggled
up in his warm,
comfy bed.
"Mmm ... cosy,"
thought Dog.

Then in
waddled
Goose.
"You look
so cosy!"
she said.

Goose nuzzled
up to Dog.

In strolled Cat.
"I'd like to be cosy
too," she said.

Cat climbed in with
Dog and Goose.

Along came some rabbits.
"We want to be cosy! Can
we be cosy too?"

The rabbits hopped in with Cat, Goose and Dog.

Mummy Bear and Baby Bear plodded along. "Can we come and cosy up with you?" they said.

Mummy Bear and Baby Bear
curled up with the rabbits,
Cat, Goose and Dog.

Then Goat and Snake arrived.
"This looks like a good
place ... to get cosy,"
they said to each other.

And Goat and Snake
wriggled in with
Mummy Bear
and Baby Bear,
the rabbits,
Cat, Goose
and Dog.

Trumpety! Trumpety!
In stomped Elephant.

"WOW, THAT'S WHAT I CALL COSY!"

he said.

So Elephant
cosied up
with Goat
and Snake,
Mummy Bear
and Baby Bear,
the rabbits,
Cat, Goose
and Dog.

Patter, patter, patter. Along came Mouse.

"How cosy..." he said.

And Mouse climbed
right onto the tip of
Elephant's trunk.

How tickly!

AAAAAAAAAAAAAA...

"SO sneezy!" miaowed Cat.
"SO noisy!" snuffled Rabbit.
"SO trumpety!" squawked Goose.
"SO scary!" gruffed Mummy Bear and Baby Bear.
"SO blowy!" yelped Goat and Snake.

And Elephant, Goat and Snake, Mummy Bear and Baby Bear, the rabbits, Cat and Goose all ran away.

All except Dog.

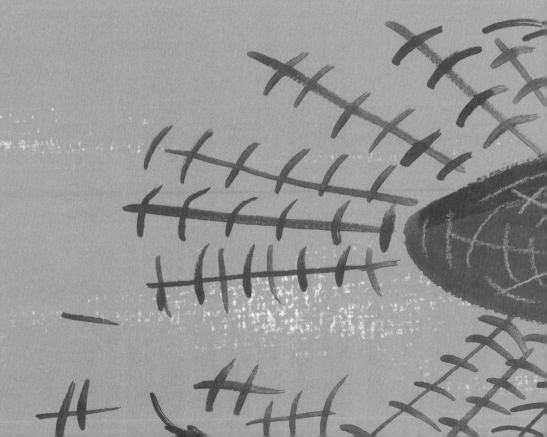

"So quiet,"
thought Dog.

Patter, patter, patter. Mouse came back. And he snuggled up with Dog in their warm, comfy bed.

"Now this really *is* cosy!" Mouse said.

"*Ever so* cosy!" said Dog.

First published 2014 by Walker Books Ltd, 87 Vauxhall Walk, London SE11 5HJ

This edition published 2015

2 4 6 8 10 9 7 5 3 1

© 2014 Lerryn Korda

The right of Lerryn Korda to be identified as author/illustrator of this work has been
asserted by her in accordance with the Copyright, Designs and Patents Act 1988

This book has been typeset in WB Korda

Printed in China

British Library Cataloguing in Publication Data:
a catalogue record for this book is available from the British Library

ISBN 978-1-4063-5998-5

www.walker.co.uk